The Pride Street Crew

4

She Likes Me!

Mike Wilson

Published in association with
The Basic Skills Agency

Acknowledgements
Cover: Stuart Williams/The Organisation.
Illustrations: Jim Eldridge.

Orders: please contact Bookpoint Ltd, 39 Milton Park, Abingdon, Oxon OX14 4TD. Telephone: (44) 01235 400414, Fax: (44) 01235 400454. Lines are open from 9.00–6.00, Monday to Saturday, with a 24 hour message answering service. Email address: orders@bookpoint.co.uk

British Library Cataloguing in Publication Data
A catalogue record for this title is available from The British Library

ISBN 0 340 74710 2

First published 1999
Impression number   10 9 8 7 6 5 4 3 2 1
Year   2004 2003 2002 2001 2000 1999

Typeset by Fakenham Photosetting Ltd, Fakenham, Norfolk
Printed in Great Britain for Hodder & Stoughton Educational, a division of Hodder Headline Plc, 338 Euston Road, London NW1 3BH by Athenaeum Press, Gateshead, Tyne & Wear.

JOHN / BONE

WESLEY / TALL

LUKE / SKY

SIMON / CUSTARD

CARL / SPOT

Carl was going away.

His Dad had a new job.
It was in New Zealand.
They were going
to New Zealand
at the end of term.

Carl told us,
'I can't take much with me.
You lot can have my things
when I go.'

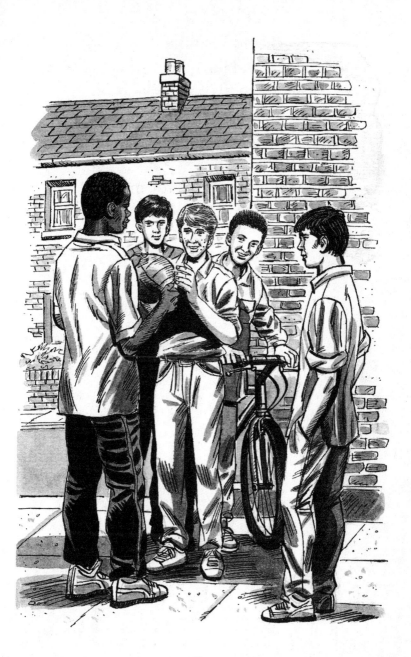

Carl sold his bike
to Dean Hardy.
He gave his football
to Wesley.
'Look after that ball, Wesley,'
said Carl.
'Get a few goals for me!'

Carl gave his Saturday job
to Sid James.

'Look after that job, Sid,' said Carl.
'It's money in your pocket.'

On Sunday afternoon,
Carl phoned me.

'Luke,' he said,
'I want you
to look after Lizzy for me
when I go.'

I said,
'You can't give away
your girlfriend
like a bike,
or a football.'

Carl said,
'I don't want her to go out
with Wimp, or Sid,
or Beany, or Pill.
I can't stand that lot!

'I want Lizzy to go out
with one of my friends.
Someone I can trust.
Someone like you, Luke.'

'I just want to know she's safe,'
Carl went on.
'I want to know
she'll be all right
when I go.

'I'm seeing Lizzy tonight,' Carl said.
'I'll tell her our plan.'

I slammed the phone down.
I said to myself:
She'll go mad.
I know she will.

I don't know
if Lizzy likes me.
She never said so.
But she'll never
go out with me now.

I always liked Lizzy.
I liked her a lot.
I always wanted
to go out with her.
But now I had no chance.

Carl had made sure of that.

The next day was Monday.
I saw Lizzy
on the way to school.
She was with Nicola Wilcox,
her best friend.

Nicola was smiling –
a girl's smile.
A secret smile.

At first, Lizzy
didn't look at me.
She didn't say hello.

Then she came over and said:

'Just what
do you think I am?
Do you think
I'm a football?
Do you think
you can pass me
from one boy to the next?'

Lizzy walked away.
Nicola Wilcox
gave me a look.
Then she ran after Lizzy.

She was still smiling
that smile.

That night, the phone rang.
Dad went.

'Luke, it's for you!' he called.
'A young lady ...'

Dad's eyes went wide.
He held the phone out.

I said, 'Hello ...'

She didn't say who it was.
But I knew who it was.

'I really liked you, Luke,' she said.
'But I can't
go out with you now,
can I?'

I looked up.
Dad was still there.
Listening.

I wanted to tell her everything.
All that came out was:
'Carl.
It was all his idea.
Not mine.'

'I know,' she said.

I waved at Dad
to go away.
But Dad just stood there.

'Andy,' said Mum.
'Come away.
Leave him alone!'
She pulled Dad
out of the room.

It was now or never.

'What are you doing
on Saturday?'
I asked her.
'Are you still going
to Carl's leaving party?'

'Yes I am,' she said.
'See you there.'
And she hung up.